Hanna & Annie,
I hope you enjoy Fritz's story!

With Best Wishes,
Anna Della Camera

Fritz

XO   XO

Fritz Goes to the Ritz ®

By Donna Della Camera and Sharon Della Camera
Principal Editors Wippleton & Waynes, UK
Copyright 2018

Churchell Hill Van Cleef Publishers, New York, NY
Belgium, Copenhagen, London, UK
Robert S. Hunt, Publisher

Illustrations by Kristina T. Lewis

Prerna Bajoria
Design and Review

CHURCHELL HILL PUBLISHERS

Fritz Goes To The Ritz

Clever Cat Publishing Group, and Co-Publisher Churchell Hill Publishers, UK Children's Book Company, New York, NY. USA

ISBN: 978-0-692-17832-4 (Hardcover)
ISBN: 978-0-692-17833-1 (ebook)

Printed in the USA

Illustrations and Art work performed by Kristina T. Lewis with permission from The Publisher and under contract by the Author's Donna and Sharon Della Camera,

Fritz Goes to the Ritz

"Fritz, Oh Fritz,
No Mom, Nor Dad.
So Sad, So Sad,
For a Havachin Lad."

Created and written by:
Donna M. Della Camera and Sharon A. Della Camera

Fritz Remembers Mom

On the corner of 6th Avenue and Central Park South in New York City you will find the Ritz Carlton Hotel at Central Park. It is a striking building, with two flags flying on opposite sides of the elaborate awning over its entrance. One is the American flag, and the other is a flag of the Ritz's beautiful Lion Crest. The Ritz Carlton Hotel is undeniably one of the most splendid places in all of Manhattan.

At the front of the Ritz, several stories above the entrance door, an adorable little dog sat looking out of the window. His name was Fritz.

It was an unusually mild, late summer day. The heavy fog was beginning to burn off, making way for the brilliant sunshine that would beam down on The Ritz Carlton. Sadly, on this particular morning, Fritz was reminded of the day, almost a year ago, when he was taken away from his real mom. Both mornings seem so similar; Fritz remembered that earlier day with a great deal of sadness. They were putting him in a cage when he saw his mom for the very last time. Fritz turned around to steal one more look at her. Though Fritz's mom knew this day would come, as it did with all her pups, she looked very, very sad. Fritz thought he almost saw a tear rolling from her eye.

His mom was a gorgeous Japanese Chin with a beautiful strawberry blond coat and glowing big brown eyes. His mom always told him how special and how handsome he was. He would miss her, and he loved her very, very much.

Then he was spirited off, in a van with some 20 or more cages holding pups of various shapes, breeds, and sizes. They drove far, far away from the puppy farm to what would become, for Fritz, the first of several pet stores.

The Pet Store and Horatio Briggs

But no one, it seemed, wanted to adopt Fritz. So he was sent from one pet store to another. Now on his fifth pet store, Fritz found himself in a pen with three other pups waiting to be adopted Chihuahua Chuck, Priscilla the Poodle, and Bichon Billy. Fritz liked Priscilla; she was the only nice one in the bunch. Chuck was really mean and intimidating. Glaring at Fritz, with eyeballs bulging out of their sockets, he'd say, "The rest of us will all be adopted, but you'll never find a home!" Billy would also join in and laugh at Fritz, although Chuck was definitely the leader. Chuck started all the trouble, all of the time. He often said to Fritz, "Where did you come from, anyway? Been around a while. You're not as young as us. What do you weigh, anyway?" Then he would tell Fritz that he was really ugly, and that was the reason no one wanted to adopt him. Chuck really liked to taunt Fritz, while Billy listened in. "You know, if you don't get adopted they'll just send you AWAY! And you know what that means, DON'T YOU?" Then he would say, "Hey Fritz, what's up with that fur of yours? Not white, not black... oh yeah, you're a Havachin! Never heard of a Havachin, have you Billy?"

Billy would then join in the mocking, "Chuck, I hav-a-chin, do you hav-a-chin?" With that, the two would just laugh hysterically. Priscilla would always tell them to leave Fritz alone, and that they weren't being nice. At least Fritz had someone who would stick up for him, but it never seemed to stop.

Fritz eventually gave up trying to defend himself. Instead, he would often stay in his corner of the pen when there were no visitors in the store. He missed his mom so much, and wanted so terribly to get out of the pen and out of that store. So when people would come into the pet store, he would try very hard to get their attention. But Chuck and Billy always managed to hog the front of the pen, and did everything they could to block Fritz from view. Chuck and Billy put on a good show, acting all sweet and lovable. Fritz wanted out of there so badly that he would hop around, hoping that someone would notice him. But Chuck and Billy always got in his way.

And it didn't really matter much anyway, because when people did notice Fritz, even they would say hurtful things about him. They would point and say, "Look at that one. He has too much energy. I bet he never sleeps."

Sometimes visitors to the pet store made fun of him for not being purebred, saying, "Why bother?" They would point at him and chuckle. Day after day, they would make comments like, "His spots are too loud, his eyes are too bright," or "His personality is just too big" and "What kind of a dog is he, anyway? A Havachin, well that's different." All of this gave Chuck and Billy even more ideas for ways to be mean to him. Priscilla would always talk to Fritz and try to make him feel better, but it just didn't help.

Eventually the others found homes, even the mean ones, but Fritz was left behind. It was especially hard for Fritz when Priscilla found a home, even though Fritz was happy for her. He really would miss her.

So Fritz found himself alone, again.

The only bright spot in his day was when Mr. Horatio Briggs would deliver pet food to the store. He was a kindly man, and Fritz liked him very much. Mr. Briggs paid special attention to Fritz and always spoke to him. He also brought him homemade peanut butter treats that his grandma, Ruby, made especially just for Fritz. Fritz really loved them. Mr. Briggs would often say to Fritz, "Don't worry little guy, you're going to find a home soon. I just know it." Fritz looked forward to seeing him each week, and they became good friends.

But as Fritz's body grew larger and his pen seemed to grow smaller, he knew he was getting older and his chances of adoption were dwindling. Fritz got sadder and sadder and started to wonder, "Why isn't anyone coming for me? I may not be all one color, or all one breed like the others, but I'm a Havachin, half Havanese and half Japanese Chin and very proud of it." "My mom told me that I have black and white fur, big brown eyes, and a beautiful, fluffy white tail, just like my dad. I wag my fluffy, white tail for everybody, even if they don't want to give me a home."

One day Fritz overheard the pet store workers talking. "He isn't selling," they said. "What are we going to do? We'll have to send him away."

Fritz knew they were talking about him, and he got very scared. He thought, "Oh no, where will they send me? I have to get out of here!" Poor Fritz. Would he ever find a home of his own?

That night he cried and cried and cried. The next day, Mr. Briggs was making a delivery to the store and saw that Fritz's big, beautiful, brown eyes were all red. He said, "Fritz, what's wrong? I have never seen you looking so sad."

Mr. Briggs was very worried and asked the store workers about Fritz. One of them said that they would have to send Fritz "away" because no one wanted him. Mr. Briggs said "Away! Where?" The store worker did not answer.

Upon overhearing this conversation, Fritz really panicked. While no one was looking, he first tried to jump out of the pen, but it was too tall. Then he hit the lock on the pen door with his paw, and it sprang open. He ran as fast as he could, right out of the back door. And once outside, he saw Mr. Briggs' truck parked with the driver's side door open, though just a bit. Fritz jumped onto the cab of the truck, then squeezed through the open door and hid as best he could under the seat.

Back inside the store, Mr. Briggs knew he had to help Fritz find a home, and fast, but he did not have a lot of money. He asked the store clerk, "How much does he cost?"

She replied, "We've marked him down to $950 dollars."

Mr. Briggs searched his pockets for money, and came up with only $54 dollars and some change. With so little money, he would have to seriously negotiate for Fritz's freedom. Mr. Briggs told her that he would be happy to take Fritz off their hands, and that they would be better off without him there, looking all sad and rejected. "Can I buy him for this?" he asked, showing her all the money he had.

The lady clerk said, "Let me ask the manager." She spoke to the manager for a while, then returned to Mr. Briggs and said, "We know you're really fond of Fritz, so yes, you can take him for only $50."

Mr. Briggs could hardly believe it, and smiled a big smile. He paid the money and then ran over to Fritz's pen, almost knocking down a shelf. But when he got to the pen, it was empty! Startled, Mr. Briggs asked, "Where could he have gone?" He and the store workers looked all over the store, but could not find Fritz.

After searching and searching, Mr. Briggs finally gave up looking. Very disappointed and sad, Mr. Briggs went back to his truck and drove away from the pet store. But then, out of the corner of his eye, he saw something fluffy and white moving under the passenger seat. He stopped the truck to look a little closer, and could see that it appeared to be a tail. No! Could it be? Only Fritz had a tail like that! "Fritz," he said, "is that you?" Fritz hopped onto the seat and gave Mr. Briggs a big sloppy kiss on his check. Mr. Briggs patted him on the head and told him, "You don't have to worry or run anymore. They let me have you, and I'm going to find you a 'forever home.'

Fritz was just ecstatic that Mr. Briggs had rescued him!

So off they drove. Then they came to a bridge, and as they drove over it, Fritz stuck his head out of the window. He could not believe how big this bridge was. People in other cars who saw him would wave and smile, and say "Hi!" or "Hello!" Everyone was so friendly! Mr. Briggs noticed Fritz's interest, and was very eager to tell him about the bridge.

"We're driving across the George Washington Bridge, Fritz. It was built in 1931, and it's been said to be one of the most beautiful bridges in the world. It has a double deck, and goes from New York all the way to New Jersey. It is 4,760 feet long." Mr. Briggs continued, "Fritz, did you know there's another great New York bridge called the Brooklyn Bridge that I cross often? You would get a fantastic view of the Statue of Liberty from there. That beautiful statue symbolizes democracy, friendship, and freedom. Sort of what you are experiencing now, Fritz. You finally have the freedom to find yourself a 'forever home.' Perhaps someday you will get to visit Lady Liberty."

Fritz Arrives at the Ritz, and Meets Eric and His Friends

They continued to drive, heading to New York City, and soon approached Manhattan. Mr. Briggs told Fritz that they were about to visit the greatest city in the world. Mr. Briggs got very animated as he tried to describe the city to Fritz. He told him what an exciting place New York City is, always busy and full of different and interesting places to see. He spoke about the many types of people of this great city, who help to make it so unique. And just like the city, they are unforgettable. "You'll see, Fritz," Mr. Briggs explained.

Mr. Briggs really loved the little guy, but he knew that his work and lifestyle would not suit his new friend Fritz, and so he wanted to find him the perfect home. He told him, "You know, Fritz, I'd adopt you, but life on the road is not the life for a sweet little guy like you." As he drove, he couldn't stop thinking of how he might find a home for Fritz. Finally, it came to him. "Of course," he thought. "I'm headed in that direction now. I know the perfect place and the perfect person to help me find Fritz a 'forever home.' Mr. Briggs' next stop was the Ritz Carlton Hotel at Central Park, where his friend Eric worked.

Once they arrived in the city, looking around in every direction, Fritz could not believe how tall the buildings were. And all the people, so many people! They all looked very different, and that did not seem to Fritz to be such a bad thing. As Mr. Briggs got closer to the Ritz Carlton Hotel, he told Fritz, "You are going to meet a very good friend of mine. His name is Eric.

Eric works at the Ritz Carlton, one of the greatest hotels in the world. The Ritz Carlton at Central Park is a masterpiece; it's simply awesome. You won't believe your eyes when you see this place, Fritz. And my friend Eric loves animals all animals, but especially dogs."

Eric was a seasoned employee of The Ritz, who was much beloved by the staff and guests alike. As they drove up, it just so happened Eric was standing at the side door. As Eric walked over to the truck, Fritz popped his head up, and Eric said, "Well, who do we have here, Horatio?" So Mr. Briggs told him that this was Fritz, and that he needed a "forever home."

"Well," Eric said, "No problem. He certainly is cute enough. Fritz is welcome to stay with me here at the Ritz Carlton until we can find him the perfect home."

"No way. Can this be?" thought Fritz. He could hardly believe what he was hearing from Mr. Briggs' friend Eric. Fritz liked Eric immediately, and he could tell that the feeling was mutual. Eric told Fritz what a very handsome dog he was, and that he liked Fritz's pretty white tail, too.

As the three of them walked to the side door of the Ritz, Eric told Mr. Briggs to bring Fritz right inside so he could show them around. Mr. Briggs told Fritz, "You don't know how lucky you just got! The Ritz Carlton is one of the most spectacular places in New York, and people come from all over the world to stay here. It really is an extraordinary hotel." Then he added, "The Ritz Carlton also has the most breathtaking views of Central Park. The rooms are magnificent and the beds are comfy, too." Fritz just LOOOOVED that!

As Fritz walked around the hotel with Eric and Mr. Briggs, it felt so magical to him. He could not believe just how great it was. Mr. Briggs was right. Eric introduced Fritz to all the people who worked there. Everyone commented on how cute Fritz was, and they were all so friendly. "Wow," Fritz thought, "I'm loving it here already!"

At one point, a well-dressed man approached Eric to thank him for the fabulous room with the stunning view. When he was out of earshot, Eric turned to Mr. Briggs and Fritz and said, "That is Ernesto, and no doubt he'll be looking for a new room within a month. He's a brilliant man, but a demanding one."

After a long day, Mr. Briggs finally said goodbye, and Eric took Fritz to get him settled in for the evening. Mr. Briggs had reassured Fritz that he would be checking in on him. But Fritz felt very secure with his new friend Eric. They went into one of the hotel's spectacular rooms, which turned out to be Eric's room which he used when he stayed at the hotel after working late. When Eric opened the door to his room, Fritz just stopped in amazement. The bed had piles of pillows and a beautiful comforter. Walking on the carpet felt like walking on a cloud. And the windows–such big, beautiful windows! They even had what Fritz would learn were telescopes. Guests could use them to catch closer views of Central Park. Fritz really wanted to try out the bed, but he was very hungry, so he waited patiently while Eric got him some dinner. Then it was bedtime for Fritz, and as he drifted off to sleep, he realized he hadn't felt this comfortable and secure since the short time he had spent with his mom.

Fritz spent several days in his luxurious room being fed fabulous food. He also took walks with Eric. During these walks, Fritz would be greeted by hellos and compliments by some of the people walking by them. Again, Mr. Briggs was right. Fritz was so impressed by the people here. They were much nicer than the visitors to the pet store.

At the Ritz, Fritz was getting to know some of the employees. His favorites were Cody, Marshall, and Marvin the Marine. Cody was a young, pretty, petite New York University student from Ohio who worked part-time at the Ritz and often took care of Fritz while Eric worked. Marshall was an occasional driver and doorman and had been in the Army. He had the blondest hair and the bluest eyes and spoke in a great southern accent.

But Fritz was especially fond of Marvin, who was retired from the Marine Corps. Marvin was the daytime doorman, and had a certain pizzazz about him. He always held the door open for Eric and Fritz when they went on their morning walks. He was a great big, chunky man with a voice so deep and rich and smooth--like velvet. Fritz would occasionally hear him sing before the lobby opened in the morning. Naturally, Marvin sang a lot of patriotic songs, and Fritz liked "America the Beautiful" the best. Marvin always smiled when he saw Fritz. He would give him a little pat on the head and tell him that he was the handsomest little fella he had ever met.

One day Fritz overheard Eric and Marvin discussing a gala which was to be held at the Ritz. Marvin was helping to promote the gala which was called the FAB Gala. The Ritz had asked Marshall to fill in for Marvin as doorman. So Marshall, in a doorman's outfit, opened the doors for the guests so that Marvin, dressed in full military uniform, could greet them and tell them about the gala. It would not have been appropriate for Marvin to be working, opening doors, while in full military uniform. But in this way, he was able to draw a lot of needed attention and promote the FAB Gala.

During that time, Fritz noticed Marvin, while in Marine uniform, making a hand gesture to the side of his forehead in return to a group of uniformed soldiers who had done the same while walking by the Ritz. Eric explained that it was a salute and also told Fritz that Marvin was a brave man, who had put his life on the line many times to protect us and to protect all of America's freedoms. Fritz was determined to salute his brave friend Marvin. He really wanted to show his appreciation, but at the same time he wanted to impress Marvin, too. Over several days and without Eric or Cody knowing, Fritz kept jumping on the bed to see himself in the mirror, trying to learn how to salute.

But it was not easy learning to salute. Fritz would stand on the bed and try to balance on three paws, while lifting his right paw off the bed and raising it up a bit. At first he couldn't manage it, and just ended up sitting down. It was definitely easier to start while sitting, so Fritz practiced the whole morning putting his right paw to his forehead.

In the afternoon, after lunch, a nap, and a walk with Cody, Fritz was back in the bedroom and up on the bed. First he practiced standing on all threes. He did this several times, without realizing how close he had gotten to the edge of the bed. And then, just when he had the salute down pat, balancing perfectly on three legs, and his paw to his forehead, OH NO! His left paw slid off the bed, and so did he.

He was a little stunned, so he took a short break before getting back on the bed again. From the center of the bed this time, he balanced on all threes and saluted again and again and again. And YES, he finally learned how to do it! It might not have been perfect to the human eye, but Fritz was surely proud of himself. Though his head ended up a little crooked and his paw looked a little flat, he could not wait to show Marvin the Marine.

So the next morning, Fritz walked with Eric, who was holding his leash, and they made their way out to the front entrance. Marshall was tending the door that day, while Marvin stood alongside him in uniform. Fritz faced Marvin as though he were at attention. Before Marvin could bend down to pat his head, Fritz stood carefully on three legs while pulling his paw to his forehead, and made a salute to his brave friend. Marshall and Eric were surprised. Marvin was definitely surprised, and also a little bit amused, because the salute was not perfect. But he didn't want to hurt Fritz's feelings. He gave Fritz a big smile and returned the salute. He then said, "Needs a bit of work, Little Soldier, but carry on."

Eric was also impressed, and said, "Yes, we'll work on that."

And if a dog could smile, Fritz would have been smiling. He knew that he had impressed Marvin the Marine, and Eric and Marshall as well.

The Sweet-voiced Lady and the FAB Gala

Now, Eric, Cody, Marvin and Marshall were not the only ones that Fritz would take a liking to.

One morning, he could hear Eric's footsteps coming down the hallway, but before he reached the door Fritz heard a voice call out, "Hello Eric, how are you?" That voice sounded like the sweetest voice Fritz had ever heard.

Eric replied, "I'm fine, Dee Dee and how are you?"

"Okay," she replied, "I'm okay"

"Are you sure?" Eric responded.

"I'll be alright." she said. "I'm headed off to the library to do some volunteer work. I teach a class for adults who can't read, so they can learn how to read. Volunteering helps to fill my day in a really positive way, you know. I just love this class, and I'm learning so much from my students at the same time. It is very fulfilling."

"How is the FAB Gala coming? Is everything all set?" asked Eric.

"Oh yes, Eric," she responded. "Many thanks to you and to the Ritz, for all your help."

"Well, I love the acronym FAB, 'For America's Bravest,' and I know how much the veterans will appreciate it," said Eric.

Dee Dee replied, "The Gala is going to benefit a very worthy cause, and a very special group of people. Well, I'll see you later, Eric." And she left for the library.

Eric finally came into his room, where he greeted Fritz with his customary big hug and kiss, and gave him his favorite breakfast, oatmeal and sweet potato tots with a little butter. Fritz gobbled everything up hungrily, and soon they were ready to take a walk. "Not too long a walk right now," Eric said to Fritz, "I'm going to start my shift soon."

While they walked, Eric wondered, who would be able to give Fritz what he needed and deserved most, a loving home of his own? Then it came to him. Of course. Dee Dee Divine. Dee Dee had been his great friend for some time now and would be the perfect forever mom for Fritz. Dee Dee came from a long line of outstanding women who were an inspiration to many. Dee Dee's grandmother, Gretel James, was a Pulitzer Prize winning author. She was also a brilliant scientist. She came to this country with only the clothes on her back. But she worked hard and didn't give up, and she became very famous and wealthy. Dee Dee's grandmother always told her, "You must always feel blessed and grateful for everything that you have and must always give to those less fortunate than you." Dee Dee loved and admired this great woman.   Besides her pretty face and scholarly knowledge of the arts, Dee Dee was indeed a very generous and kind person.

They left the Ritz and walked down Central Park South to Fifth Avenue among the hustle and bustle of the busy sidewalks. So many grand shops, such wonderful aromas from the restaurants. "Is there anything this city doesn't have?" thought Fritz. But if Fritz actually could speak to Eric, what he really wanted to ask him was, who was the sweet-sounding lady that

Eric had greeted in the hallway that morning? Though he loved his mornings and walks with Eric, Fritz had become very curious on the Sweet-voiced Lady.

They weren't very far down the block when a man called out, "Yoo hoo, Yooo hooo, Eric! Oh, Eric!" It was Ernesto, one of the guests of the Ritz Carlton. Surprised to see Eric walking a dog, he said, "Eric, I didn't know you had a puppy."

"Oh, no, Ernesto," Eric replied. "I am just caring for this pup, Fritz, while I try to find him a 'forever home.'

"Oh, really," Ernesto responded.

Ernesto was a world famous designer, and very flamboyant. He had a slight build, and shiny, dark hair. As always, he was very well dressed. Today he wore a deep gray suit with a bright pink shirt. After Eric introduced the two, Ernesto bent down and made a light, little pat-pat on Fritz's head and said, "Lovely little doll, aren't you?"

"Sure, Ernesto. But I thought you loved the morning sunlight. Didn't you say that it inspires your creativity?"

"Well now, Eric, that was last week, and this is this week. I would rather have the afternoon sun now. Be a doll, won't you?" Ernesto replied.

Eric answered him, "Okay, we'll find you a room facing west."

"Outstanding!" Ernesto responded. "That's why I love the Ritz so much.

The staff here is simply tremendous! Not to mention how beautiful the place is! Pleased, Ernesto said "Well remember, Eric, if you or the Ritz ever need anything, a favor, keep me in mind. Ciao." And he left.

Except for his fabulous black leather shoes, which looked delicious to nibble on, Fritz was a little puzzled by Ernesto. Eric and Fritz continued their walk, eventually returning to the hotel.

Back at the Ritz, Eric lets Fritz roam about, but reminded him not to get into mischief. While Eric was working, he had Cody keep an eye on him. Fritz wandered the lobby and hallways, marveling at the columns and marble floors. Fritz then jumped on the elevator along with several hotel guests, who commented on how beautiful the little Havachin was. Once again, if dogs could smile, Fritz would have been smiling at that moment.

Before you know it, Fritz arrived on his own floor, so he got off the elevator to do some investigating.

Just as luck would have it, he approached the door to the Sweet-voiced Lady's hotel room and it was unlocked. Standing on his hind legs, using both front paws, and after trying several times, Fritz managed to open the door and got into the room.

"Wow, oh wow!" he thought to himself. "This room is fantastic! Everything, the windows, the drapes, the furniture, the chair." He noticed a picture frame turned face down on the dresser, but for now he headed for the closet, and what a closet it was! It had so many clothes, gowns, and shoes, so many beautiful shoes. He took several and admired them. Before long, he began to nibble on them.

Suddenly, he heard the door open, and so he ran from the closet and scrambled underneath the bed. The Lady was back. "I knew I forgot something," she muttered to herself. She had left her handbag, and she began walking around the room, looking and looking for the bag. From under the bed, Fritz finally saw her for the first time. He couldn't believe his eyes.

"Oh wow!" he said to himself again "I've never seen a prettier lady in my life. Her hair is so long and so, so red--just beautiful." The Sweet-voiced

Lady finally found her purse, but did not spot Fritz, who was still hiding under the bed. He was simply in awe of the lovely sight he had just seen, and made up his mind that he had to meet the Sweet-voiced Lady.

It wasn't long before Cody came looking for him. As Cody was calling for him in the hallway, Fritz made a mad dash out of the room where he had been hiding, and stood in front of the door to Eric's room. He had forgotten to return the shoes to the closet. But Cody had her back to him, so for now, Fritz had managed to go undetected in his mission to investigate the Sweet-voiced Lady.

All he knew right then was her name was Dee Dee, and that she was pretty and had fabulous red hair, but he knew, just knew, that she must be a kind and gentle person.

The next morning, Fritz sat looking out of the window with its view of Central Park. He had mastered the use of the telescope, which gave him a bird's eye view of the park below. Cars and people and horse-drawn carriages seemed to be everywhere. With his keen canine hearing, in the midst of all the goings-on, he heard a man call out. "Lady Divine, Lady

Divine, would you like to partake of a ride with me in my carriage?" As Fritz peeked through the telescope, he saw Dee Dee and a tall man with fuzzy brown hair who was speaking to her. He was dressed in a green plaid shirt and blue shorts, and wore a light green fedora with a brown feather on his head. He was riding a bicycle, which was attached to a carriage. Eric had mentioned on one of their walks that they were called rickshaws.

"No thanks, Rick," said Dee Dee. "I am going to walk today. It's great exercise, and it's a positively beautiful day. Anyway, the library isn't far from here."

Rick shouted out to her again, "As long as you're keeping it Green, Lady Divine, keeping it Green!"

Dee Dee turned around and answered with a big grin. "Yes. For my health, and for the ENVIRONMENT!" But then she switched subjects. "By the way, Rick, I'm not a princess or a queen. Please just call me Dee Dee."

Rick chuckled and said, "Ahh, but you will always be a grand lady to me, L–a–d–y D–i–v–i–n–e." With that Dee Dee smiled, shook her head and turned to walk in the opposite direction down Central Park South. Then she turned onto Fifth Avenue.

"Okay," Fritz thought to himself, "I have to get into that room again, the room with all of those shoes belonging to Dee Dee Divine." But how was he going to pull it off?

Fritz wanted desperately to meet Ms. Divine, and he was going to try his best to make a good impression. Fritz had grown to love Eric, and he knew the feeling was mutual, but he understood that Eric could not give him a 'forever home.'

Then Fritz thought, "I'd better take a nap and rest up because aside from getting out of the pet store this is my greatest challenge ever." He was drifting off to sleep, when he heard Eric's voice in the hallway.

"Hi, Horatio, I'm fine and so is Fritz." He continued. "I've been meaning to ask you if you know of anyone who would like to adopt Fritz. He can only stay here a month or so more, unless he's adopted by a permanent resident."

When he overheard this, Fritz began feeling very nervous. He knew he could not stay forever at the Ritz, but could this be happening again? His mind was racing and his heart was pounding. When and how and where was he going to make his grand first impression on Ms. Divine?

And if he did meet her, would she like him or even want to be his forever mom? While he had many new friends, how could he get them to help win Ms. Divine's heart? So far it seemed no one wanted to adopt Fritz. Alone again... Where would he go?

Fritz was so scared and upset that he did not hear the end of the conversation. He didn't hear Eric tell Mr. Briggs that he had devised a clever plan to get Ms. Divine to adopt Fritz if she hesitated. But, of course, he was not 100 percent sure that the plan would work.

Fritz had to think fast. Should he run for it and go out on his own? Very sad and exhausted, he put his head down on his bed as Eric entered the room. He pretended to be asleep; he couldn't act as if everything were okay. Eric went over to Fritz and assumed he was asleep. He gave him a kiss and a pat on the head and then left.

Then Fritz drifted off into a deep, deep sleep...

Time passed, and Fritz realized it was already dark out. He must have slept for a long while. His thoughts immediately went back to his dilemma. Eric had tried to find him a forever home, and it just wasn't working. Fritz believed that now he was becoming a burden to Eric. Dee Dee would be a great forever mom, but what if she did not want to give him a home? `He began to cry; he felt so hurt and alone. Panicked, he thought he couldn't take any chances and knew what he had to do. He had to leave.

He turned to look one last time at the room he found so comfortable and secure. He would really miss it. Down the hall he snuck onto the elevator; luckily it was empty. Once in the lobby he did not see anyone he knew, so Fritz snuck out of the very back door he first came into with Eric. He knew Marvin was probably manning the door up front. Once outside, he looked around in every direction. "Which way should I go?" he thought."

It was dark and scary and beginning to rain. He ran to the street and tried to blend into the crowd. The streets were really busy. He was getting wet, and it was hard to see, and people were walking by him at a quick pace.

Just as he started across the busy avenue, he felt someone touch him and then pick him up. At first he thought it was Marshall because it was a tall man, and he seemed so strong. But then he heard a nasal, sinister, high-pitched voice and knew it was a stranger.

"Well, well, well, and where might you be headed?" the stranger asked.

"Oh, no," Fritz thought as he struggled to be free of the man's grip.

The man just laughed and said, "Feisty little one, aren't we?" Then he added with a sinister chuckle, "Gee, you got no identification. I wonder who you belong to."

Fritz continued to struggle to free himself and thought, "I'm big now and don't need anybody."

But the stranger held firm and said with a frightening tone, "I bet you're not pedigreed, so you won't fetch a good price. But I know where you will be of some use, and at least I'll make a little something."

Fritz was struggling. He was trying to get away, but it was no use; the man was too strong. He didn't need to see the man's face to know that he was mean and really terrifying. He continued to carry Fritz to the back door of a van. The man was strong and quick and really good at doing this sort of thing. It probably was not his first time.

As they approached the van, Fritz heard those voices. "No way, it can't be!" he thought. "I know those voices and those laughs. I'll never forget those laughs."

The stranger opened the door. Then Fritz saw them. They were in separate cages that were labeled 'PUREBREED'. It was Chuck the Chihuahua and Bichon Billy. Frantic, Fritz tried with all of his might to get free, but he couldn't. Then he was carelessly tossed into a cage. He managed to see what his cage was labeled before he was tossed into it. It said "MUTT!"

Then Chuck said, "Look at you Fritz. Nobody wants you. You are gigantic. You can't even fit in your cage."

Billy was laughing, saying, "Yeah, the Havachin has a chin alright—try a few chins." They were both laughing and glaring at him.

Chuck continued to taunt Fritz. "Guess what Fritz? We are going to great homes with big yards to run around in and guess where you are going?"

And as they continued to tease Fritz, the van took off with the stranger driving. It was moving faster and faster and faster until it felt to Fritz that it had lifted up and was flying through the air. Fritz managed to look out of the back window and could see down onto the street. He saw people walking in different directions and the tops of buildings as the van flew higher and higher. Then he saw the roof of the Ritz. And on the roof stood Eric, Mr. Briggs, Marvin the Marine, Marshall, and Dee Dee Divine. They were waving for him to come back, shouting, "No, Fritz. No! Come back!" And their faces grew smaller and smaller, and the van flew higher and farther away from them. Fritz jumped around and pushed against the door of the cage, frantically trying to get out. He tried and tried to get out of the cage and out of the van. But it was no use. Fritz could not escape.

Then he heard Chuck, Billy, and the stranger again. They were all laughing at Fritz. As Chuck moved closer to him, his eyeballs bulging, he said in a menacing tone, "And guess where you're going Fritz? YOU ARE GOING FAR, FAR AWAY!"

"Fritz, Oh Fritz!

No Longer at the Ritz.

Why Couldn't He Stay?

Now He's Gone Far, Far Away."

To be continued....

Acknowledgement

Firstly, we would like to thank our parents, Margaret and James Della Camera. Our mother Margaret, for sharing her love of words and writing. She inspired us with her creativity, wisdom and altruistic spirit. Our mom's unconditional love was never in question.

Our father James, for sharing his love and zest for life. He had that rare ability to light up a room with his uncanny persona. Our dad epitomized confidence, hard work and determination.

Together, they both instilled in us the importance of respect, consideration and the act of kindness which they believed could never be too small. Through their example, we learned the importance of these virtues, as well as, a love for animals. Without living by our parent's example this book would not be possible.

They are dearly missed; always in our hearts.

A very special thanks to Robert S. Hunt of Clever Cat Churchell Hill Publishing for believing in this project and making it come to fruition. We would also like to thank Kristina T. Lewis, illustrator, with her brilliant talent for capturing the true quintessence of Fritz and Nancy Silva, editor, for her expertise in polishing our manuscript.

Lastly, to Fritz, the sweetest and sloppiest kisser on 4 legs and the inspiration for this story.

It was love at first sight and Fritz is truly loved, unconditionally.

CPSIA information can be obtained
at www.ICGtesting.com
Printed in the USA
LVHW060858051118
595972LV00003B/16/P